Kids love reading
Choose Your Own Adventure®!

"I love the way the you can choose your own adventure and that the author makes you feel like you are the characters."

Shannon McDonnell, age 10

"I think these books are great! I really like getting to be one of the characters."

Ahn Jacobson, age 11

"I think that this book was very exciting and it is fun to chose your ending. These books are great for all ages to."

Logan Volpe, age 12

"I think these books are cool because you actually get involved with them."

Melanie Armstrong, age 12

"I think *Choose Your Own Adventure* books are thrilling. I also like the way you change the way the story ends."

Molly Mobley, Age 9

"They have a mystery to them that makes it fun to read. I like being able to solve them my own way. They have different endings which make me want to read them more."

Gabe Pribil, Age 10

TERROR ON THE TITANIC

BY JIM WALLACE

ILLUSTRATED BY SITTISAN SUNDARAVEJ
COVER ILLUSTRATED BY NATHAN BARCHUS

CHOOSECO®
WAITSFIELD, VERMONT

Terror on the Titanic ©1996 R. A. Montgomery/Ganesh, Inc., Warren, Vermont. All Rights Reserved

Artwork, design, and revised text ©2011 Chooseco LLC, Waitsfield Vermont. All Rights Reserved.

Illustrated by: Sittisan Sundaravej and Kriangsak Thongmoon
Cover Illustrated by: Nathan Barchus
Book design: Stacey Boyd, Big Eyedea Visual Design

For information regarding permission, write to:

CHOOSECO
P.O. Box 46
Waitsfield, Vermont 05673
www.cyoa.com

ISBN-10 1-933390-24-7
ISBN-13 978-1-933390-24-6

Published simultaneously in the United States and Canada

Printed in Canada

0 9 8 7 6 5 4 3 2

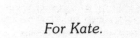

For Kate.

BEWARE and WARNING!

This book is different from other books.

You and YOU ALONE are in charge of what happens in this story.

There are dangers, choices, adventures, and consequences. YOU must use all of your numerous talents and much of your enormous intelligence. The wrong decision could end in disaster—even death. But, don't despair. At anytime, YOU can go back and make another choice, alter the path of your story, and change its result.

It is April 10, 1912 and you are headed from London to continue studies as a classical pianist. You've already garnered quite a bit of prestige, so your hopes are high. You are traveling on the RMS *Titanic* under the supervision of your father's business associate, Andrew Tempkin. However, your faith in this large ship's infallibility is quickly to be deterred, as this crew is much too distracted to notice impending icebergs! You'll have to be on your toes every second, or else this voyage is going to end much more abruptly than you had planned—in the icy northern waters of the Atlantic ocean!

You stand on the deck of the RMS *Titanic*, the brand-new White Star ocean liner. She's the biggest, most luxurious ship in the world, and she's on her first voyage across the ocean, from Southampton, England to New York City. The date is April 10, 1912.

The ship has just pulled away from Southampton quay and is moving into the River Test. A huge crowd walks along the quay, following the great ship's progress down the narrow river channel.

The *Titanic* glides by the *New York*, a smaller ocean liner moored at the side of the river. You watch as the smaller ship is sucked toward the *Titanic*. Bang! Bang! Bang! You hear several loud reports, like gunshots. Looking down, you see the ropes holding the moored ship arc high into the air. They must have snapped! The *New York* begins to swing away from her mooring directly toward the *Titanic*!

You gasp and grab the railing, expecting a shuddering impact. As you watch, the *Titanic* slows to a drifting stop, and the bow of the New York swings past her port side. A collision is narrowly avoided.

"That was a close one," says a tall, gaunt man standing next to you. He has a pale, lined face with a thin, grim mouth. He speaks with a lilting Scottish accent. "It's a bad way to begin a maiden voyage. A bad omen."

Turn to page 2.

"Bad omen! Pah!" says a middle-aged Englishman standing nearby. A watch chain hangs from the brocade waistcoat buttoned tightly around his stout middle. He sports great gray muttonchop whiskers. "There's nothing to fear! The technical journals I've read say she's unsinkable. She's a wonder ship!"

"Aye," sighs the tall man knowingly. "She is indeed a wonder ship, a mighty ship. But the ocean is mightier still. Many a mighty ship has kissed the bottom of the sea." With that, the man turns and walks slowly away.

"Don't listen to him," says the Englishman. "This ship is beautifully engineered. I tell you, she can't sink."

Turn to the next page.

4

"She is beautiful and enormous," you say, gazing up admiringly. The *Titanic* is nine hundred feet long and has four huge funnels. Her hull is painted a shiny black and her deck superstructure is white; her yellow funnels with black tips rise sixty feet above her top deck. It does seem unbelievable that such a massive ship could sink to the bottom of the ocean. Still, the Scotsman's comment has chilled you.

"Oh, so you're an American!" says the Englishman. He extends his hand. "The name is Stites. Were you on holiday in England?"

"No," you say, shaking his hand. "I've been in London for the past month, studying classical piano."

"A classical pianist, eh?" says Mr. Stites. "So you've been in England alone, then?"

"No. My father was with me. He has an import-export business. He had to stay in London to meet a client. I'm returning to New York with his partner."

"Import-export business, you say. Would the name of your father's partner be Andrew Tempkin?" asks Mr. Stites. You nod. "Yes, I met the chap just before we boarded. He told me he bought himself a black Rolls-Royce."

"Yes—it's onboard. He's taking it back to New York," you say.

Go on to the next page.

"You know, you should meet my daughter, Jessica," says Mr. Stites. "She's just your age and a very agreeable lass. I'm sure the two of you will get along famously. She had a go-round with the violin for a time, but science is her wicket. That's where the future's headed, you know. She'll be good company for the voyage."

Mr. Stites' mention of Andrew gets you thinking about him and the gold Buddha statues that he and your father imported from Siam. The box containing the statues arrived at the office in London while your father was out. Andrew was excited but seemed hesitant to open it in your presence. He asked you to run an errand. When you came back, your father had returned, and he and Andrew were examining the two statues, each about a foot high. They seemed disappointed. The workmanship was poor. Worse, the statues weren't solid gold but made of lead painted with gold leaf. Your father grew angry and vowed he'd get even with the Siamese trader who cheated him.

Andrew supported your father and agreed the trader was a scoundrel. Something about his manner made you suspicious. In contrast to your father's genuine rage, Andrew's reaction seemed mild. You don't trust him, and you aren't happy to be sharing this transatlantic journey with him.

Turn to page 7.

Over the next few days, you and Jessica Stites
explore the ship. It's like an immense, fancy
floating hotel. There's a Turkish bath, a swimming
pool, a squash court, a gymnasium, a barbershop,
a hospital, a post office, and several restaurants
and cafes.

Late Sunday evening, about eleven-thirty, you
and Jessica are in the first-class lounge on A Deck.
You've been there for a couple of hours playing
cards. Abruptly, Jessica puts her cards down.

"I'm bored playing gin rummy." She folds her
arms and pouts. Jessica is bright and generally
agreeable, but you realize she's a little spoiled.

"That game was getting boring, especially
because you kept winning. Let's go out on deck
and see what's going on up forward," you suggest.

"Same ocean up there that's back here," she
answers, still wearing that pouty look.

"Then how about the Marconi Room where the
radio transmitter is?" you ask. "I know one of the
men who operates the radio there. Wait'll you see
it—it's huge!"

That does perk her interest. "I know Morse
code, did you know that? My father bet I couldn't
learn it and I did!"

Turn to page 8.

8

The Marconi Room, the radio shack, is up forward on the port, or left, side of the ship. To get there you walk along the deck to the other end of the ship. You and Jessica shiver in the arctic air. Overhead the night sky blazes with stars; below, the ocean is glassy smooth. You're amazed at how calm the water is. There's not a ripple.

Yesterday afternoon Harold, one of the two radio operators, met you as he was leaving the shack. He invited you to drop by anytime. Without knocking, you open the door and go in, Jessica behind you. A smell of hot electrical insulation hangs in the air. A man is on duty, but it's not Harold.

"Mind if we watch a minute?" you ask.

The operator doesn't hear you, or if he does, he's too busy to reply. He's wearing earphones and staring intently at a stack of papers. A blue spark flashes between the contacts of the radiotelegraph key he's tapping with his index finger. You're entranced by the rhythmic Morse code and the sparking light. The message sounds important, but you can't understand it.

Jessica does, though. You watch her concentrate on the pulsing beeps as you both stand nervously just inside the door.

Turn to page 10.

10

Suddenly an incoming signal blares from the earphones so loudly you can hear it across the room. The operator tears the earphones from his head and smacks the stack of paper. With an exasperated look, he raps back a message. He spots you and says, "Not now, too busy. Later. Out, please."

You both nod and duck out the door. Jessica grabs your arm. "That was weird. Those were private messages he was sending, maybe to a land station for relaying. Messages like 'Meet you Wednesday noon at the Waldorf-Astoria.' Then a signal came in. He got flustered and told the guy to shut up and keep the air clear. Another ship must be nearby."

"What was the other ship saying?" you ask.

"I couldn't get the first part. Something like 'stopped, surrounded by ice,'" Jessica says.

"Ice! Icebergs!" you say. "Maybe we're coming into an ice field. Let's go on deck. We may be able to spot some."

"Icebergs! I'm cold enough already. I'd rather go visit my friend the chief baker," Jessica says. "He's baking bread right now. Think of it—hot, fresh bread . . ."

"Oh, come on, be a good sport! Let's see if we can spot a few icebergs, then we'll warm up at the baker's," you say. Jessica reluctantly agrees. "I'll get the binoculars and meet you on the promenade deck," you add.

Turn to page 16.

"Ahoy, crow's nest!" you cry your loudest. You wonder if "ahoy" is the right word. You shout a couple of times; the rushing air muffles your voice. They can't hear you shouting from the promenade deck.

You rush down two decks to get to the well deck and then run forward till you're almost underneath the crow's nest mast. It looms far above you.

"Iceberg, iceberg!" you scream up at them. At your shout, one lookout peers intently into the distance, then clangs the warning bell three times and speaks urgently into a telephone.

It seems like an hour goes by. Nothing happens. You can't feel the slightest change in the rhythm of the *Titanic*'s engines or sense the deck move under your feet the way it should when the ship changes course. And because you're down in the forward well-deck area, with the forecastle blocking your view, you can't see the iceberg, either.

Just as you sense the turning of the bow under your feet, a shower of ice cascades over the starboard well-deck rail. One of the huge pieces brushes you and slides with a thump into the stairway you just came down.

Turn to page 19.

12

You decide to let the mystery in Andrew's car go for the moment. No one can leave the ship until it docks in New York in a couple of days, so it can wait.

Jessica is squatting behind the promenade-deck railing where it curves around the forward section of the ship on the starboard side. You stand under the bridge with a clear view of the crow's nest, and beyond it, the bow. You hand her the binoculars.

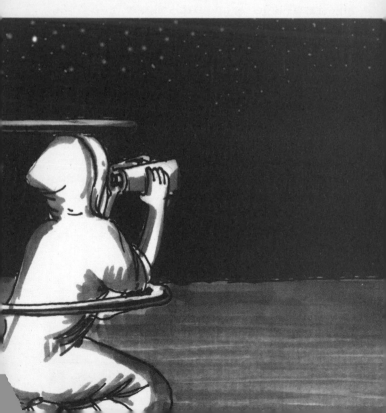

"It's beastly cold," she chatters after a couple of minutes. "I can't see any more with these than I can without them. Just smooth black sea. I'm turning in." She hands the binoculars to you and leaves.

For a couple of minutes, you sweep the horizon in front of the *Titanic*. Just as Jessica said, there's nothing but darkness. The stars look brighter through the binoculars, though. The great bronze capstans near the bow glint under the stars. You train your gaze on the two lookouts more than thirty feet above you up in the crow's nest. Funny, they don't have binoculars.

You sweep the horizon another time. You catch a point of light that shimmers faintly. It's duller than starlight. Maybe it's a reflection?

Turn to page 15.

You strain to see. It's massive, filling the view of your binoculars, but fixed, so it can't be another sea craft . . . . It glows eerily against the dark sea. The starlight bounces off its reflective edges so that it looks as lit up as a small city in the distance. It's an iceberg!

"Wow!" you gasp. The lookouts are staring right in its direction, but they can't see it without binoculars.

You keep watching as the iceberg gets bigger. Do you dare run up to the bridge, where no passengers are allowed, and warn the officer on duty? Or should you tip off the lookouts and let them deal with it? Maybe you should wait a little until it can be seen more clearly.

If you go directly to the bridge, turn to page 24.

If you call to the lookouts, turn to page 11.

If you take time to make sure it's an iceberg before going for help, turn to page 21.

16

You zip down the stairs to the stateroom you're sharing with Andrew. It's on B Deck, a couple of decks below on the port side. As you reach your cabin door, you hear a loud voice inside: ". . . safest there, I tell you! No one will think of a car's frame—" The voice stops short as you knock a couple of times and enter.

Andrew is talking to a dark-haired man. They both look at you sharply. "Sorry, just want to get these," you say. You grab the binoculars from the table and leave.

As soon as you're outside, you grimace with disgust. The man is Oscar Kilpatrick, a friend of Andrew's. He got on the *Titanic* at Queenstown, Ireland, on Thursday afternoon. You don't like him. When he boarded, he greeted Andrew but ignored your offer to shake his hand.

Turn to page 18.

18

You're still angry about the brushoff—that and the man's arrogant and patronizing manner. You have as little trust in Oscar as you do in Andrew. You don't understand why your father chose Andrew as a partner. Sure, he's sharp in business, a real smooth operator. But that's the problem. He's a little too sharp.

You stop walking and think, *What's in the frame of Andrew's car? Safe from what?* Andrew's Rolls is in forward hold No. 2, way down on G Deck near the bow. You're headed that way.

If you postpone meeting Jessica to explore Andrew's car, turn to page 42.

If you go to meet Jessica with the binoculars, turn to page 12.

The *Titanic* limps at half speed into New York, two days late. Damage below the starboard water-line has kept all its pumps working continuously. Hull plates on three of the forward watertight compartments are badly smashed by the brush with the iceberg.

Your steward saves a great chunk of ice in the ship's refrigerated storage for you. You show it to the *New York Times* reporter after the *Titanic* docks. You and your ice end up in a front page picture.

The End

You need some more time. It may be a mirage. Or maybe it's a cloud.

To get a better view you run up the steep stairway leading from the promenade deck to the boat deck. Before you get there, three distinct rings from the lookouts' warning bell tell you they've spotted something.

You see a huge iceberg looming in the darkness ahead, and coming closer. There's a slight, grinding noise as the *Titanic* brushes the iceberg, and then it's over; the iceberg glides swiftly out of sight into the darkness astern. You hear something crash onto a deck below.

You poke at the ice that's down in the well deck, then push the forecastle door open. Maybe you can find out if any water is leaking into the ship near the bow where the berg struck.

It's quiet. The constant humming and jangling vibration of the ship's woodwork and glass fixtures has stopped. That's strange. You peer down the forecastle spiral stairs.

Three or four decks below, a big blond man with a couple of companions starts climbing the stairs. His feet and legs are dripping, and he's carrying his belongings.

"Ship taking water?" you call out.

"Right she is!" he yells up, with a Swedish accent.

Turn to page 22.

22

A nervous thrill runs through you at his words, then your heart jumps when you see a tumble of bright green seawater foam around the spiral stairway several decks beneath him. The *Titanic* is in trouble.

"Come! We're going to the stern. It's dry there," he shouts. He beckons to you to follow. You've never met this man, but you immediately trust him.

It's a long trek along the E Deck passageway to the stern. The man shows you into the third-class smoking room. Pine paneling covers the walls. Your friend finds the bar closed, so he persuades someone to start playing dance tunes on the piano.

A cluster of men, women, and children swarm into the large room carrying water-soaked baggage; some of them are crying. Your friend and the others laugh at the new group and begin a circle dance around them to try and cheer them up.

Weird, you think. The ship has hit an iceberg! And no one's doing a thing.

You leave and go forward toward the lifeboats. A crowd of people is gathered in the first-class lounge, laughing and joking. The entire ship's band is even playing some lively ragtime music. *Don't these people know what's going on?* you wonder, really confused.

Go on to the next page.

Near lifeboat No. 3 on the forward starboard boat deck, First Officer Murdoch is talking to Captain Smith. Some men are uncovering the lifeboats. A group of passengers, some with life belts on, stands around.

"Women and children first," says Officer Murdoch as the captain goes off to the bridge. Murdoch stands near a boat and motions the women passengers on while more people slowly appear on the deck from their cabins below. Excitement is in the air—at least something is happening. The boat is now half full of women and children. A few men even get in!

"You with the binoculars—know anything about open boats? We're short of crew on No. 7 here. I want to send her down now," Murdoch says, looking at you.

If you say, "Yes, I do," and step forward, turn to page 90.

If you say, "I think I'd do better helping load boats," turn to page 81.

24

You ignore your fear, running up the steps to the bridge on the topmost deck. It's called the boat deck, and it's where the lifeboats are. You're in luck. First Officer Murdoch, who let you look at the bridge the other night, is on duty.

"Sir," you say, gasping for breath as you open the door, "iceberg!" You point dead ahead.

Murdoch whips his binoculars up, stares intently for a second, and leaps to the wheelhouse. "Hard a-starboard!" he commands the man at the wheel.

Your heart pounds. From inside the bridge, you watch the dark mass grow distinct through your binoculars. Clear now is the triangular peak that you saw reflecting the starlight; it's getting bigger. Half a minute goes by, and still the *Titanic* hasn't begun to turn. Then two things happen.

Clang! Clang! Clang! The bronze bell in the crow's nest rings three times. They've spotted the danger.

And then the ship's bow starts to move slowly to port. You watch it trace a smooth arc against a few low-hanging stars near the horizon. Your mouth opens; the iceberg's tip looks as high as the *Titanic*'s bridge. It seems certain that the ship is going to smash into the looming, glistening mountain of ice.

Go on to the next page.

A few seconds later the bow clears the iceberg, and the *Titanic* surges past it.

"Lord! Narrow shave," the junior officer on the bridge mutters shakily.

Murdoch walks over to you and says, "I shall commend your action to the captain." You're not certain what that means.

"Just luck, I guess," you say, trying to cover up the fact you're breathing hard from excitement and fear. "Should the ship go slower tonight? If there are more icebergs—"

"Thanks. Visibility is excellent tonight. Time for you to leave now. We've work to do," he says with a smile.

As you leave, you overhear him tell a man who's just come on the bridge, "Mr. Olliver, take these glasses to Fleet and Lee in the crow's nest."

Turn to page 26.

The next evening, you're sitting at the captain's table as a guest of honor along with Andrew and your friend Jessica. The table is in a recessed bay of the huge first-class dining room. The room is beautiful, with splendid white walls and a molded ceiling.

The captain is an old, white-haired man with a full beard. His voice is soft, low, and reassuring. Also at the table is a quiet man, Mr. Ismay, head of the White Star Line. He and the captain have promised you a special tour of the *Titanic* from stem to stern, all decks, with an engineer to answer your questions about the super powerful steam engines.

The whole evening seems unreal. But soon you and Jessica become bored with the polite conversation. You've got something else on your mind anyway: the mystery of what's in Andrew's car.

This has been bothering you ever since you overheard Andrew and Oscar's conversation. Whatever it is, you suspect it's illegal. Andrew seems nervous. He's talking loudly to Mr. Ismay about a shipment of his and your father's.

Turn to the next page.

Over at another table you see Oscar Kilpatrick. He looks nervous too. Dinner's over. You're trying to figure out the best way to get a look at that car. First you have to find out something.

"Captain, sir, when do you expect us to dock in New York City?" you ask.

"Tuesday evening," he answers. "We're making good time—again, thanks to you."

Tuesday evening! That's tomorrow night—earlier than expected. It doesn't give you much time to search the car. During a pause in the conversation, you and Jessica politely excuse yourselves and leave.

Go on to the next page.

"Jessica, tonight's the night to explore Andrew's car," you say outside the dining room. "We may dock tomorrow night."

"I'm ready," says Jessica. She slips back to her father's cabin to get his new battery-powered light.

You meet Jessica at the forecastle entrance and descend the spiral staircase to the car hold, five decks below the entrance. It's quiet in the hold, with only the steady hum of the ship's engines vibrating the deck.

You locate Andrew's black Rolls-Royce and, with the help of Jessica's flashlight and the car's tool kit, explore the frame. On the driver's side you discover two oblong objects wrapped in white cloth. You manage to slide one out of the frame. It lands on the wood deck with a dull thud. Jessica pulls the wrapping off to reveal a gleaming metal bar.

Turn to page 30.

"It's gold!" you exclaim.

"Gold! What's Andrew doing with gold hidden in his car?" Jessica asks.

"I think I know," you reply. "I think the gold is my father's. We'd better get the other one out and take them with us."

"But what will we do with them? And what do you mean, you think the gold belongs to your father?" she asks.

"I'll explain later. Help me get the other one out. I don't think Andrew will have a chance to check the car before the ship docks." You're sure the bars are from the gold statues. Andrew probably replaced the real statues with lead counterfeits, then melted the originals down into these ingots. Now he's trying to smuggle them into the United States. And somehow Oscar's involved in this scam.

Go on to the next page.

"But the bars are too heavy to carry," protests Jessica. "And what if Oscar or Andrew does decide to check the car? We could be in big trouble."

She's right. The bars are heavy, and you're not sure where to hide them. On the other hand, few people are wandering around this late at night; no one is likely to see you. You need just ten minutes or less to get the bars out of the hold and into a safe place above decks.

If you take the gold ingots out of the car hold, turn to page 36.

If you leave the gold in the Rolls, turn to page 32.

You decide it's safer to leave the gold where you found it. But it's not as easy to get the gold bar back inside the car's frame as it was to pull it out. While Jessica holds the light, you struggle and push. It's an awkward position, and your arms are getting tired.

Then you think you hear footsteps. "What's that?" you whisper to Jessica. You can't see from your position under the car.

"Someone's come into the hold," Jessica whispers back.

"Quick, turn off the flashlight and crawl under the car!" you whisper.

The two of you huddle together under the Rolls-

Royce, not daring to breathe.

The footsteps grow louder. A pair of men's shoes stops right next to the Rolls. You recognize Andrew's brown and white wing tips!

You hear him talking to himself quietly.

"What a beautiful car," he murmurs.

He nonchalantly leans against it.

"And about to make me incredibly wealthy!" he adds incriminatingly.

Will this ever end? you think. Finally he finishes.

You're about to breathe a sigh of relief when Jessica makes a noise, trying to stifle a sneeze.

Turn to page 35.

Instantly Andrew is kneeling down, peering under the car. "What? Who's there? What are you doing under my car?"

You're still holding the gold ingot. You'll have to tell him the truth.

You tell him about the conversation you overheard between him and Oscar but leave out the part about your suspicions concerning the gold Buddha statues.

"I was just curious to find out what was in your car," you say. "I was trying to get the gold back in the frame when you came in."

Andrew looks at you coolly for a moment. "Okay," he finally says. "I believe you. But I better not catch you snooping around this hold again. And you better not breathe a word of this to anyone, or you might just have an unfortunate accident. Do you get my meaning?"

You nod vigorously.

"I'll be watching you," he adds as you and Jessica leave the hold.

You still hope to get a message back to your father about the gold once the ship docks in New York. But it's going to be difficult with Andrew and Oscar watching your every move.

The End

"Even if Andrew and Oscar check the car and find the gold missing, there's no reason they would suspect us," you reassure Jessica. "Besides, once the ship docks, we may never get another chance to get the gold."

You and Jessica each take a bar and slip it under your jackets.

"We can't risk hiding them in our cabins. Let's stash them in one of the lifeboats," you say.

It's difficult keeping the heavy bar hidden under your jacket as you ascend the spiral staircase. You climb three more flights to reach the boat deck where the lifeboats are located. It's on a level with the bridge. A short distance down the deck you see a figure emerge from a doorway.

"Quick!" you whisper to Jessica. "We've got to dump this gold." You shove the ingots under the canvas covering of the lifeboat nearest you.

"Hey there!" says the man. You recognize the voice—it's Oscar! "What are you two doing here? I thought you'd gone to bed."

"We decided to stroll around the ship first," you say, trying to sound nonchalant.

"Why're you hanging around the lifeboats?" Oscar asks. He sounds suspicious.

"We were just checking out the davits, to see how they work," you say. "Well, we're going to turn in. See you later." You hurry away with Jessica.

Go on to the next page.

"Phew, that was close!" you say to Jessica when you're out of Oscar's earshot.

"Do you think he saw the ingots?" Jessica asks.

"No, it was too dark," you say, with more confidence than you feel.

"How are we going to get the gold when the ship docks tomorrow?" asks Jessica.

"When the first-class passengers are lining up to disembark, meet me by the lifeboat with a small carrying case," you say. "We'll each carry off an ingot as part of our luggage. Just be sure not to let anyone touch your case."

When you dock, everything goes as planned. There is just one moment of panic when Oscar offers to carry your case, but you insist on carrying it yourself. You just hope you haven't aroused his suspicions by being too insistent.

Turn to page 39.

You, Andrew, Jessica, and her father are staying at the Waldorf-Astoria. You arrange to stay with Jessica and her father, figuring it's a safer place for you and the gold.

On your first night, Mr. Stites goes to visit a friend. You and Jessica stay behind in the hotel room to discuss what to do with the gold.

"I think I should telegram my father and tell him what's happening," you say.

There's a knock at the door. You exchange glances. Neither of you is expecting anyone. The knock is repeated. Cautiously you open the door a crack.

The first thing you see is the dull glare of a pistol, followed by Oscar's hoglike face. His angry sneer reveals confidence that he's about to get what he wants.

"I think you'd better let me in," he says.

Turn to page 40.

40

"Okay, kid, where's the gold?" Oscar growls. "And don't play dumb. I know you've got it here."

You nod to Jessica, who opens her case, revealing the bar of gold. Oscar immediately strides over to examine it. For a moment, he stands with his back to you, ignoring you. You creep up behind him with your case containing the other ingot and, with all your strength, strike him on the back of the head.

He instantly crumples to the floor.

"Time to call the police," you say to Jessica, "and explain everything."

Andrew and Oscar are arrested for grand larceny. You receive commendation for your role in saving the *Titanic* and for your brave actions leading to the arrest of the criminals. Best of all, your father agrees to split the profits from the sale of the gold with you, and you are able to buy the grand piano of your dreams!

The End

You must save the gold! This could be your only chance. You push open the car-hold door.

You kneel down by the Rolls. It takes you a couple of minutes to unbolt the plate and pull one gold bar from underneath the car. You set it on the front seat. The bars weigh so much you can only carry one.

Wham! Something smacks the back of your head.

You awake slumped in the car's front seat. Your head is throbbing. The gold is gone. Your knees are being lapped by icy cold, foamy seawater.

Holding your head, you stand up slowly and swish through the numbing water to the door. It's locked. You pound and pound and yell for help until you're hoarse. No one comes.

The water is up to your waist now and still rising. You climb onto the roof of the car. Was the door locked on purpose to help save the ship from flooding, or to keep you in? You wonder as you wait and the water continues to rise.

The End

You hurry to the forward well deck, which shelters you from the icy air, and cross to the forecastle entrance up near the bow. You descend a steep spiral stairway and reach the car hold, five decks below the forecastle entrance.

Inside the hold it's quiet and smells of motor oil. Light gleams off the black Rolls-Royce. Thick ropes around each axle anchor the car securely to the hold deck. You look around. You seem to be alone.

You explore the car's frame. It's made of large, pipelike tubes. On the driver's side you spot a metal end plate that seals one of the hollow tubes. You find a wrench in the car's tool kit, remove the bolts, and pull the plate off. You strain to see inside. It's too dark. You light a match. The flame reveals a foreign object lodged inside.

You barely make out two rectangular objects wrapped in white cloth. The match dies, and you only have two more. You find a wire and manage to hook one bundle and gently tug it up the frame tube. It falls onto the deck, with a dull thud. Some of the cloth rips away.

The next match you light reveals a bar of shiny metal almost a foot long. "Gold!" you whisper to yourself. "It's a gold ingot!"

Turn to page 44.

44

What are gold ingots doing in Andrew's car? Then it comes to you. Of course! The gold Buddha statues were fakes! These must be the real statues. Andrew is the one who swapped the gold statues with counterfeits and then had the original statues melted down into bars. And now he's smuggling them into the United States. The ingots are too big and heavy for you to lug away alone. You decide to replace the gold bar and get above deck where you belong.

You pause for a second: are those footsteps you hear approaching? Your heart beats hard. No one comes. You rewrap the ingot. You kneel, half under the car, stuff the ingot back in the frame, and bolt the plate on.

Braang!!! A deafening noise and shock wave reverberate through the car hold. The sound is like a huge steel vault door banging shut—but it lasts longer, tapering off into a series of rending, ripping sounds. A shuddering vibration lifts the car body above you.

Turn to page 50.

As you and Jessica climb the forecastle spiral staircase, a rat scurries down onto the deck and vanishes behind a capstan.

"Where's the car?" asks Jessica.

"On G Deck, I think. But look! It's too late—it's partly underwater." You wade along the passageway on G Deck to the car hold. Icy water curls around your knees. The door won't budge.

"Hey, grab the mail!" A group of postal clerks beckon to you.

"We hauled all the sacks up from the deck below to this sorting room," one of them says. "Now this deck's flooding. Wish they'd get those pumps working."

"Here, help us with these," says another clerk to you and Jessica.

Turn to page 55.

You hesitate, your hand on the door. You sense no vibration, none of the humming sounds a powered steamship makes. The engines must have stopped, you think. "Stopped, surrounded by ice," was the message that the other ship radioed. Did the *Titanic* hit an iceberg?

You leap up the forecastle stairway to look for Jessica. Two crew members hurry down the stairs.

"That iceberg was as tall as the ship."

"Lucky we just nicked it."

"Check the bow compartments and back to the boiler rooms. We may be taking water."

"Not likely. The iceberg just grazed her."

That's what you think! you think. *She's taking lots of water.*

On the well deck, the open area between the *Titanic*'s superstructure and the forecastle, you spot Jessica. She and some others are playing soccer with a chunk of ice. There must be tons of ice lying in heaps on the well deck.

Jessica kicks a big chunk to you. "Where have you been? Where are the binoculars you were going to get? You should have seen that iceberg the ship hit! It was huge!"

"I left the binoculars down below," you say. You pull her aside and tell her about the gold in the Rolls's frame. Jets of steam are blasting out of the escape pipes mounted on the three forward funnels. You guess the ship is releasing pressure in the boilers now that the engines are stopped.

"You don't say!" Jessica exclaims. "Gold! What are you going to do about it?"

Turn to page 48.

"I'd like to get it back to my father, somehow," you say. "Or at least let him know that Andrew's cheating him."

"Well," says Jessica, "we could go back to the car and get the gold out. I'd like to see those gold bricks!"

"Yes, but I don't want to draw attention to ourselves," you say. "I don't want Andrew or Oscar getting suspicious. Anyway, this iceberg hit seems kind of serious. Why are we stopped?"

The *Titanic* is motionless. Passengers up on the promenade deck walk along arm in arm, talking and laughing and pointing at the ice in the well deck where you're standing. Two girls are having a snowball fight with chunks of ice. Plumes of steam rise high above the resting ship.

The roar of escaping steam sounds ominous, as though the ship were in pain. What should you do?

If you return to the car with Jessica, turn to page 45.

If you ask Jessica to explore aft along the passenger decks with you, turn to page 52.

You never forget the eerily calm night the *Titanic* sank. You don't forget the sounds the helpless people in the water made. Of the eighteen lifeboats that were launched that night, only your lifeboat and one other went back to help. The others, most of them with extra room, just rested their oars.

The End

50

You scream and cover your head with your hands. But the car body settles back without touching you. Feeling foolish, you roll out from under the car and run to the forecastle stairway.

Did the *Titanic* hit something? The sound came from below. You rush down the stairs to explore. Below is another cargo deck. You open the door and see large, neatly stacked cases. You don't know what you're looking for, but you feel a vague dread. You descend to the bottom of the stairs. Now you're at the bottom of the ship. A sign on the door says FIREMEN'S PASSAGE. CREW ONLY.

When you open it, you hear a hissing and gurgling. Water! A man hurries toward you along the passageway from the boiler rooms. Foaming green seawater is rising above the walkway.

Sloshing through the swirling water, the man shouts, "She's taking water clear back to No. 5 boiler room! She's a goner, mate. Better clear out!"

You run up the stairs after him. At the car hold door, you pause. The gold! Should you save it? Or should you get up on deck?

If you open the car hold door and try to salvage the gold, turn to page 41.

If you continue up the stairs to the well deck to find Jessica and see what's happening up there, turn to page 46.

"Jessica," you say, "water's rising down in the car hold. It's too risky. Let's see if we can find an officer and get some information. Maybe it's serious. Why else would they stop the ship?"

You climb up to the starboard promenade deck. Through the windows of the smoking room you see groups of men laughing and talking. No one's even looking outside. You can't find any officers, so Jessica goes to find her family. You stop by your cabin. Andrew's in bed.

"Andrew, you'd better get up!" you say, jostling him awake. "We've hit an iceberg. It doesn't look good. A lot of water is coming in."

"Huh? An iceberg? I didn't feel a thing, and I'm a light sleeper," he says, sitting up on the edge of the bed. "Don't worry. This ship's supposed to be unsinkable."

"Better get ready, just in case," you say. "Maybe you should check with our steward if you can find him. I'll try to find out as much as I can."

You think of going directly to the bridge this time, even though it's not allowed. Your hunch is that the man from the boiler room who told you the *Titanic*'s a goner is right, but no one else seems to know or care.

High up on the top deck, the boat deck, is the bridge, the *Titanic*'s command post. It's also where the lifeboats sit. You peer into a half-open window of the enclosed part of the bridge. Captain Smith and another man are examining a blueprint. You remain silent.

Go on to the next page.

"Well, sir, I give her an hour, an hour and a half at most," says the man, who looks familiar to you.

"I'll order the lifeboats readied," says Captain Smith.

"Lifeboat capacity is about one thousand. There are more than two thousand people aboard," the man says.

"Women and children first," says the captain. A man approaches the bridge and you slip away in the other direction, horrified at the information you've just overheard.

Your hunch was right. The *Titanic* is doomed, and there's not enough lifeboat space for everyone. Your watch says fifteen minutes past midnight. It's been about half an hour since the *Titanic* hit the iceberg.

Turn to page 54.

54

You feel numb. You can't believe that this wonder ship is going to sink. It feels like a rock under your feet. It's so big, and the sea's so calm.

Walking down several decks aft toward Jessica's cabin, you know it's true: the *Titanic* is sinking. What can you do if there aren't enough lifeboats?

You recall suddenly who that man with Captain Smith is. He's the ship's engineer. He showed you around the ship's workshop. You saw carpentry supplies—planks, rope, and barrels. With help, you could build a decent raft in under an hour.

Outside Jessica's cabin you feel a flutter of panic. She's not there. Maybe there's no time to build the raft, and you should just concentrate on finding your friend.

If you look for Jessica in the Marconi Room up on the boat deck, turn to page 59.

If you head for the workshop to start building the raft, turn to page 57.

You make a trip up to F Deck carrying the heavy mail sacks and hurry back down to G. You run into the mail sorting room and slosh toward the last dry bag of mail on the table. The overhead lights are steady and bright. It's so strange to see important letters and packages floating around!

A crumbling sound rumbles through the room. The ship's bow drops lower in a sudden motion.

"Watch out!" cries Jessica behind you.

A wall of water and heavy wet mailbags slams into you, forcing the door shut and pinning you to the floor. You fumble through the dark water, blindly searching for Jessica, a postal clerk, anything to hold onto but the cold sea.

The End

On your way to the workshop you decide to stop at the baker's. You might be able to get some provisions for your raft.

You descend the first-class staircase, go through a door, and down more stairs to the vast kitchens on D Deck amidships. The smell of fresh bread starts your mouth watering.

"There aren't enough lifeboats. I'm going to build a raft. Could you spare some bread?" you ask a burly man pulling a batch of bread out of the oven.

"A raft? Sounds a bit far-fetched to me," says the baker. "We're taking this bread up to stock the boats, but I can give you a loaf. Good luck."

As you start to leave with the loaf tucked under your arm, a voice calls out from behind, "Hey, mate, that raft sounds like a good idea to me." You turn to see one of the bakers walking toward you.

"Mind if I join you? It may be the only way out for the likes of us. Name's McCracken," he says. You shake the floury hand he extends to you.

Turn to page 58.

58

"Yes, I can use your help, Mr. McCracken," you say. "Come on." On the way to your stateroom you hear a voice boom, "Women and children in the boats first, please." It sounds like it's coming through a megaphone way up forward.

"Hey, where have you been? Scrounging for bread at a time like this? You don't mind if I have a piece, do you?" asks Jessica. She and Andrew are standing just outside the stateroom door. You introduce them to McCracken and outline your plan.

Jessica says she'll help with the raft. Her father has gone up to the lifeboats.

Andrew, up and dressed now, says, "I've checked with one of the ship's officers. You're right—it's women and children first, and there aren't enough lifeboats. I'm for the raft. I don't think the *Titanic* will sink, but just in case. No one can live long in the North Atlantic. That freezing water is certain death."

Turn to page 69.

Jessica's not on the boat deck. You check your watch. It's twenty minutes past midnight.

You knock on the door to the radio room and push it open. "Hello," you say to the operator. "Did my friend come by?"

He shakes his head.

"We've hit an iceberg. It's serious, I think. The boat is taking a lot of water along the bow," you say.

"Harold, hear that?" the operator shouts. "That bump was an iceberg!"

A curtain inside parts and Harold appears, buttoning up his shirt. "Ho, then there's work for us tonight," he says. "Might have to head back to Belfast for repairs."

The captain steps into the doorway. You quickly move aside. "Send a distress signal. Here's our position," he says and hands over a slip of paper.

"Captain!" You rush to join him as he leaves. "Is it serious? It looked bad in the forward cargo hold."

"You're everywhere, aren't you?" he says. "Yes, it's bad. If you want to help, give a hand with loading the lifeboats down there. Women and children first. Under no circumstances suggest the ship is sinking. We may have a panic on our hands. Clear?"

Turn to page 60.

"Yes sir!" you answer.

An officer struggling up the steep stairs to the bridge with a large metal case calls out to you.

"Give us a hand up these steps. This climb's about finished me," he says.

You hesitate. You've got an important assignment from the Captain. If you're going to delay his orders, the officer had better have something urgent going on.

If you give him a hand and continue on to the boats, turn to page 61.

If you give him a hand and ask what's in the metal case, turn to page 64.

"Okay," you say, and grab a handle. Together you slide the case up the stairs and carry it to the open part of the bridge. The heavy case reminds you of the hidden gold. You leave the bridge and cut a message with your knife in the soft brass metal of the plaque on the door to the stairway. Above and below the words THIS DOOR FOR USE OF CREW ONLY, you carve GOLD IN ROLLS-ROYCE IN HOLD, APRIL 15, 1912.

You rush over to the other side of the boat deck, hoping no one saw you. What if the *Titanic* doesn't sink and someone finds the message?

You're engulfed by frightened passengers, shouting officers, and sweating crew. You work your way through the crowd. It surges aft until you're by lifeboat No. 13. You wonder if Jessica's near and push closer to the boat.

"Let go of me! I won't go in that boat. Let go," says one woman.

"Lady," says a steward trying to help her, "we all have to go. You may as well go quietly."

The woman pulls away, pushes back to the first-class staircase, and disappears.

Beside you, a girl who's been looking over the *Titanic*'s rail at a lifeboat descending to the water begins to cry.

Turn to page 62.

"My mother's in that boat. I didn't have time to get in," she says, turning to you.

You grab her hand, push through to the officer loading No. 13, and explain.

"Get in now," he yells to you both.

As soon as you scramble into the boat, it begins to descend to the water.

Directly in the lifeboat's path, about twenty feet below the rail, a spout of water three feet in diameter foams from the *Titanic*'s side!

Turn to page 72.

You climb atop the officers' quarters and help sling the heavy, awkward collapsible canvas lifeboat down to the boat deck. Someone's propped oars against the wall to make a slide to the deck.

You hold an oar in place. An edge of the boat gouges your shoulder when a man on the roof lets go too soon. You get a bad flesh wound. The boat flops onto the deck with a splat, right side up.

Everyone's hurrying and getting in each other's way. Someone is attaching lines to the launching davits.

"Watch out!" a crewman on the roof yells.

A wave sweeps you and the people rigging the boat away. The *Titanic*'s bridge has just been flooded with water, and the wave tangles you and another guy together underwater. You push free with a kick and pop to the surface. Your life belt is ripped from your body, and the icy water shoots pain through you.

You catch a glimpse of something flat in the water. The ship's lights illuminate it. It's the collapsible boat you were struggling with. Feebly you get to it and hold on to its wooden rail. It's half filled with water.

With your last bit of strength, you hoist your numb body into the collapsible and lie half in and half out of the water pooled in the bottom of the boat. Maybe a rescue ship will come by soon. You hope so.

The End

"What's in the case?" you gasp, as you plunk your end down on the bridge deck.

"Rockets," he answers. "Bigger than the ones they use for your Independence Day. Distress signals to ships in the area. See those lights? They're masthead lights on a steamer standing off from us."

You help set a long rocket in a launching shoot. The officer fits a detonator to it.

"Stand clear; hold your ears," he says and pulls the firing cord.

The thunder of the rocket's launching detonator smacks your ears. Tadoom! The blinding blue-white light of the explosion illuminates startled faces further aft by the lifeboats. A delicate arc of white sparks traces the rocket's path above the *Titanic*. It explodes with a bass boom and a white flash. Smaller clusters of blazing white lights drift to the sea.

"Wow, that is better than the Fourth of July!" you say.

"Got any colored ones?" a voice comes from the stairway.

"Jessica! Come here," you yell. "Look at the ship's lights. We're trying to send a signal."

Turn to page 66.

"Set the next rocket to fire," the officer says to you. "Detonators are over there. Be careful. I'm going to signal that ship with the Morse light."

Jessica helps and decodes out loud the message the officer is sending in Morse code. The signaler looks like a winking searchlight.

"Struck iceberg. Lifeboats ready to go," says Jessica, watching the flashes.

A band of curious onlookers has gathered to watch the rocket show. The captain comes and gives an order; the officer turns to you and Jessica.

"I'm to take a lifeboat. Carry on with the rockets, one every five minutes," he says, patting you on the back as he leaves.

Funny, you think. No one in charge on the whole *Titanic* seems to have a plan for saving the passengers. Now this guy sticks you with his job. The rocket signals are important, you know. But so is your life.

If you leave with Jessica and let someone else worry about the rockets, turn to page 74.

If you stick with setting off rockets, turn to page 97.

You start shouting. Soon many voices take up the chant. "Stop lowering!" Other voices merge in, trying to name the descending boat's number. Different voices call out different commands.

A crewman tries to cut the fall lines. Another tries to push the boat away from the ship with an oar.

People are screaming in both boats just before they collide. Your boat is crushed and shoved underwater.

The End

It takes you, Andrew, Jessica, and McCracken half an hour to haul a pile of planks, hammers, nails, and barrels for flotation up to the aft well deck. It's the best place to build a raft—the *Titanic* is sinking bow first. The aft well deck is open, near the supplies, and a good location to launch the raft from. The *Titanic*'s bow is noticeably lower now, and the well deck is slowly tipping to one side.

"She's listing to port now," Jessica says. She nails a large platform of planks she's laid out to four cross-timbers.

"Everyone's below decks back here," you say. "It's weird."

"What's going on down there?" says a loud voice from the aft bridge that runs along the poop deck in the stern. It's Quartermaster Rowe, one of the ship's helmsmen.

Turn to page 70.

"We're building a raft. There aren't enough lifeboats, sir," says McCracken.

"Lifeboats! What? No one's told me anything. However, that's ship's property you're using. You're unauthorized to do that," he says. He looks angry.

"Call the bridge, sir," you shout up to him. "We hit an iceberg an hour ago. Look—there's a lifeboat."

You point to the starboard side of the well deck. A lifeboat drifts slowly astern, illuminated by blazing lights from the *Titanic*'s upper decks.

"My God," says the quartermaster and picks up the aft bridge telephone. A moment later he rushes off the bridge, goes below, and disappears forward carrying a metal case.

"Communication could be better on this ship," says McCracken.

"Well, what we have to figure out now is how to get this monster over the side without smashing it or having it fall into the water upside down," you say.

McCracken, Andrew, and you fit empty wooden barrels under the platform and lash them on with rope passed through some metal rings Andrew found in the workshop.

"Nothing says we can't use that cargo crane up there," says McCracken. "It's the latest thing. Run by electricity." He points to one of the cranes near the raft. Its hook hangs high above you.

Go on to the next page.

"Can you run it?" you ask.

"My bunkmate's the one who runs it. I've watched him," says McCracken.

You wonder about the wisdom of getting the raft into the water by using the crane. It's risky. Running the crane may draw too much attention to your project and someone could interfere.

You could just wait and let the *Titanic* sink out from under the raft. But the ship could take such an angle as it sinks that the raft might get tangled or mashed against something on deck.

If you ask McCracken to run the crane, turn to page 93.

If you decide to wait and let the raft float free from the ship naturally, turn to page 76.

72

You point to the spout of water and yell, "Watch out!"

You try to shove the lifeboat away from the *Titanic*'s side with an oar. The water is rushing strong enough to sink your boat!

"Push clear!" you shout.

Several more people pick up oars and together you shove the boat out enough to clear the water spout. Your lifeboat lands safely and drifts back along the ship's side.

"Look out above!" calls one of the crewmen in the boat as another lifeboat starts to descend. Your boat has drifted into its path. The fall lines that lowered you are still attached to your boat, holding it in position.

If you yell out, "Stop lowering,"
turn to page 67.

If you take your knife and cut the fall lines
free, turn to page 78.

"Let's go back, Jessica," you say.

You ask the captain to get someone else to fire the rockets. Then you and Jessica head for the boat deck.

The deck's angle is steep, and the people crowding it are wearing life belts. They look worried—kids holding on to their mothers, some people getting in boats, some holding back and clinging to each other.

"I've got to find my father!" Jessica says. She finds her steward on deck and asks about him. The steward urges you both to get into lifeboats and won't answer your questions.

"What do we do now?" asks Jessica. You're standing by the starboard rail, watching the last boat leave.

The *Titanic* is clearly doomed. The water is about ten feet from the rail. Far forward near the bow, the last of the forecastle has sunk, its lights glowing green through the water.

"Let's jump and swim to those lifeboats," you say, pointing to several boats visible on the smooth water. The stars twinkle on its surface.

"No. I can't swim that well," Jessica says. "Let's wait."

You say nothing. The sea starts pouring into the deck below through the observation windows.

"Okay, now," says Jessica.

"Wait!" you yell and grab at her. She falls into the water alongside the ship. It swirls in a whirlpool as it slices through the windows.

Go on to the next page.

You plunge in after Jessica and grab her life belt. For a moment you keep her from being sucked through the window into the sinking ship. Then you have to let go, and you're sucked in too.

The End

"I think it's too risky to hoist the raft," you say. "Let's wait for the ship to sink enough to float it."

Andrew disappears and Jessica runs up to the boat deck to see if she can find her father.

Ka-boom! A white distress rocket launches into the sky, leaving a silver tracing line that arcs above the radio antenna wires between the fore and aft masts. It explodes and sends soft white stars of light into the black sky. That makes six of those, you think.

"The ship's tilting up so high we can't use the crane now anyway," you say. The stern keeps mounting steadily higher. The well deck forward bulkhead is nearly horizontal, as the deck the raft is on rises to vertical.

You and McCracken shift your footing to this bulkhead and get ready to brace the raft and keep it from tipping over until the sea can flow onto the deck and float it.

"Lash the raft to the deck. That'll keep it from flipping over," says McCracken. "We'll cut it loose when it floats free."

If you agree and help McCracken tie the raft, turn to page 98.

If you tell him, "Let's wait it out; the water's almost here," turn to page 106.

"Take it easy, take it easy," you say, moving slowly toward the boat.

"Don't shoot the poor men!" says a girl in the lifeboat. She starts to cry. People standing around begin murmuring encouragement.

Staying out of Murdoch's line of fire, you take a slow step toward the two men. You try to keep a calm tone in your voice. "Look, there's another collapsible boat up on the roof of the officers' quarters," you say and point to it.

Never mind that it will be impossible to get it down and launch it before the deck itself dips under the approaching water.

Without a word, the men begin to move. Murdoch pockets his revolver. Several men rush to the boat, grab the two stowaways, and drag them out.

Murdoch motions to you and says, "Thanks. What are you doing here? Thought I sent you off in a boat half an hour ago."

"There's plenty of time left, sir," you say.

"Mind checking steerage—third class?" he asks. "Bring up any women and children left. We'll work on getting that collapsible up there launched by the time you return. Better hurry."

You find a group of young people at the front of the main third-class staircase under the poop deck. But by the time you persuade a few of them to join you, the *Titanic* has begun its great slide beneath the sea. A pocket of air remains in the stairway for several minutes as the ship accelerates toward the bottom.

The End

78

"Row, paddle, push—we gotta get out of here," you yell, stumbling over people to get to the fall lines. You hack them apart, and your boat glides clear just as the descending boat splashes into the dark sea.

Six hours later you're falling asleep in a warm berth on board the *Carpathia*, a liner that rescues the *Titanic*'s lifeboats.

The girl has found her mother and Andrew has found you. To your horror, you later learn that as many as 1,500 people have died, most frozen in the sea. You are one of 705 survivors.

Four days later in New York, you're first off the *Carpathia*, thanks to Andrew's connections. A taxi whisks you to the Waldorf-Astoria Hotel. It's late at night. You're overwhelmed by the tragedy and excitement of the *Titanic* disaster.

A frantic commotion builds outside your hotel room door. The phone rings. It's the press calling you, pounding on your door.

"Please, I must get an interview."

"Five hundred dollars for five minutes!"

"Open up! We know you're there."

"You're the first to be interviewed!"

Go on to the next page.

Wearily you open the door. You explain that you are exhausted, you don't want any money, you have a concert to do in a couple of days, and the only thing you want is some peace and quiet. It's not as though you've had time to practice. You shut the door and wonder how your performance will go, in the wake of this terrible disaster. Perhaps, you think, it will inspire a particularly tragic piece of music. You sit in front of a blank piece of sheet music and begin to write.

The End

"I think I'd help more by loading boats," you tell Officer Murdoch.

"Go below to Decks B and C amidships and tell passengers to put on their life belts and report here to boat deck. Do it calmly--no one must be alarmed. And get one yourself," Murdoch advises.

Moving quickly along the corridors of B Deck you knock on one stateroom door after another. Some people are awake, but many have gone to bed. It's well after midnight. You keep missing your step, sliding to the left. The ship's beginning to list.

"Hello, hello!" you call out as you stride along the passageway. "First Officer Murdoch wants everyone on the boat deck. Wear your life belts, please. There's been an accident. This is just a precaution."

A man hears you and waits for you outside his door. "I knew something had happened," he says. "This rumbling sound shook me awake, and a moment later some ice tumbled in my open porthole. Look," he says, and shows you a piece.

"Better get up to boat deck, sir, with your life belt," you say. "Please tell your friends."

Down on C Deck, you knock on a door and run through your routine once again. Click! You hear the door lock.

"Go away!" a woman's voice says from behind the door.

Turn to page 82.

"Ma'am, we're in danger. The ship's badly damaged. You should get topside. Captain's order—for your safety," you say.

"Who are you? Leave us alone, or I'll call our steward," a man's deep voice shouts.

"Just don't ask him to mop up the seawater when it starts pouring into your room," you snap back.

You head back up to the boat deck. From the A Deck lounge, lively music, a ragtime number, pours out along the promenade. What's going on now on this crazy ship? you wonder as you poke your head in.

Men, women, and children are moving restlessly around like a crowd after a school football game. No one's paying attention to the band or their music.

The band takes a break, and you tell the piano player how serious the damage to the *Titanic* is.

He shrugs and says, "Best to keep playing. It will keep our minds off it, whatever happens."

When you reach the boat deck again, many more people are there, and they look more serious and nervous than the group who got into lifeboats earlier. Almost all wear life belts.

Turn to page 84.

You begin helping women into one of the lifeboats. Some refuse to leave their husbands and remain on deck.

"Go ahead, dear. I hear several ships are coming soon to take the rest of us. You must get in," says a man to his wife.

You stand in the lifeboat to help those who are having a hard time crossing the gap between the ship and the boat.

A man pushes through the crowd to hand you a folded piece of paper. Then he's roughly yanked back.

Go on to the next page.

You unfold the paper and glance at it:

Tell my sister Mabel Nappi of New York City. Lost. J. H. Williams

After the boat you were loading is lowered, you locate the man standing alone and dejected by an empty boat davit. "Better give this to someone else," you say. "I'm here for a while, like you." He looks like the card shark you saw winning Saturday night in the smoking room. You hand back the piece of paper.

It's about half past one in the morning. Most of the lifeboats have left the starboard side of the ship. The band has moved up to the foyer of the Grand Staircase that connects the decks. You notice a couple of the musicians have life belts on now. They're playing louder, too. You recognize the melody. Music has been your life, yet it all seems so unimportant right now.

You go to the port side to see what's happening over there; maybe more people are getting into boats.

Turn to page 86.

86

You push through the people in the staircase foyer to the port boat deck. It looks empty; then you hear voices over the rail. You lean over it and look. They're loading another lifeboat, No. 4, from the deck below, A Deck. You go down and watch. The *Titanic* has listed so far to port that the lifeboat has swung clear of the side by several feet. Soon you're helping pile deck chairs across the gap to make a flimsy bridge to the lifeboat. You help a man across: You hand him up, then steady his legs as he teeters over.

Crack! You hear a gunshot from the starboard side!

Go on to the next page.

On the forward starboard boat deck, the last lifeboat is loading. It's smaller than the regular boats, with a plank bottom and canvas sides. Crew members have raised its sides and set it in the davits nearest the bridge.

Officer Murdoch is pointing a revolver at two men crouched in the boat. "Get out. Clear out now," he's shouting at them.

"What's going on?" you whisper to a man in the tense knot of people—all men—on the deck.

"A couple of cowards jumped into the lifeboat," he says. "The officer fired a shot in the air."

The two men in the boat freeze. One of them begins to whimper.

"Come out now or by God I'll shoot you!" Murdoch yells, his face red. You have to act fast, you can tell Murdoch is serious.

If you say something to persuade the men in the lifeboat to get out, turn to page 77.

If you hold your breath and watch, turn to page 88.

You hesitate, losing the courage to speak up. Murdoch steps toward the two men. One of them crawls under a seat. Sailors drag them both out amid the screams of several women in the boat.

You stand back against the officers' quarters and watch this last lifeboat slip down to the water as the crew plays out her lines through the davit pulleys. Fear floods you.

You go to the rail. The collapsible lifeboat that just went down is floating near the *Titanic*. The rowers are just getting their oars in the water.

Those left on deck are running toward the stern to get away from the water sweeping in at the bow. A few have climbed to the roof of the officers' quarters with Murdoch and are struggling to free the other collapsible boat. It may be your last chance to save yourself.

But you could jump into the water near the lifeboat and hope they'll pick you up. You feel ashamed of that idea, thinking of the men who were dragged from the boat minutes ago. But there are some male passengers in it. Maybe no one will figure out what you're doing.

If you jump into the sea and swim to the lifeboat, turn to page 89.

If you stay aboard the Titanic, *turn to page 63.*

You jump feet first into the black water. It's a drop of no more than ten feet, but the cold shock is like a blow.

The sound gets the attention of the people in the lifeboat. They stop rowing. You reach them and shout, "Help me!" Someone pulls you in and throws a blanket over you. You shiver on the bottom of the boat.

You are one of the lucky rescued, but the tragedy of the event and the ghosts of those lost haunt you and your music for the rest of your life.

The End

You step forward. "Yes, I do."

Hands help you up over the rail into lifeboat No. 7. The seaman from the *Titanic* in charge of the boat tells you to stand in the center while he fits the plug—which covers the boat's rainwater drain—into the boat's bottom.

You feel a quick flood of fear; you wish you were back on the ship with all the people and music and bright lights. You peer over the side. It looks like a million feet to the glassy sea below. And you feel funny about being the first to leave. What if it's a false alarm? What about Jessica and Andrew?

"It's a long way down, about seventy feet. Not to worry, we'll make it," the seaman says to you.

Turn to page 92.

The order is given; crewmen on the deck pull on lines, and the lifeboat swings out on its davits clear of the *Titanic* in a series of alarming jerks. Crewmen struggle to lower the bow and stern fall lines evenly to the water, but it's hard to do.

The lifeboat tips so low on the bow end that everyone aboard starts screaming.

"Less bow line!" you shout until they eventually stop letting it out.

On the water, you start pulling on one of the four oars. It's hard work. No one is used to such a large, open boat. It is supposed to hold about sixty-five people, but the boat's only half full.

"Hold the blade of the oar like this," you show a young woman sitting across from you.

"Thanks. I'm just so nervous!" she says. "Do you think the *Titanic* is really going to sink?"

A sharp explosion rips over the still waters. From the bridge a white rocket sails up and arcs through the night. It detonates with a boom and sends out a cluster of white twinkling stars.

Turn to page 110.

"Okay, let's hoist it with the crane," you say.

McCracken releases the storage tie-downs. Jessica rigs some lines from each corner of the raft to meet over its center.

McCracken swings the cargo crane over the raft. All you hear is the whirr of its gears; the electric motor is quiet. He lowers the crane's boom and poises it over the raft. Jessica grabs the hook and loops the lines over it.

"Take it up," you yell and jump onto the raft. You steady yourself by grabbing the lines that join in a pyramid above your head.

You're afraid the whole thing will tip and dump you. But McCracken is smooth and miraculously the raft lifts, levels, and gently descends clear of the *Titanic*'s side. The lit portholes blink by you as you glide gently onto the water.

"Hold it! Perfect!" you shout up to McCracken. "Slide down the lines. The *Titanic*'s sinking fast!"

Turn to page 95.

The water rises to one of the open portholes in front of you and flows inside in a silver cascade.

"Jessica, see if you can find your father. We have to unhook the raft soon!" you call. She takes off.

Along with McCracken, a crowd of people appear at the rail, some holding children. "Come on," you motion to them,

Jessica slides down with her father and says, "Andrew's brought a friend."

At the rail Oscar Kilpatrick is motioning to you. He and Andrew are holding a fat leather satchel with a line tied around it, which they have begun lowering to you.

Turn to page 96.

"Okay, okay, I see you," you call. "Lower away and get down here." The bag is heavy; you're sure some of the gold is in it. For the first time, Oscar acknowledges you with a nod of thanks. He's shaking with fear. Others leap into the water and climb onto the raft.

The raft floats well on the glassy water. You cast off the lines to the hook.

"Let's get out of here," says Jessica. "The ship will suck us down as it sinks."

You realize in horror that you have nothing to paddle with. Everyone frantically tries paddling with their hands and feet, but the raft stays glued to the side of the ship.

Something bounces off the raft. Startled, you look up. Towering 150 feet straight above you and tipping over the raft is the *Titanic*'s stern. It's vertical, pointing straight up at the sky.

Everyone's looking up.

"She's going to crush us!"

"Help my daughter!"

"Jump!"

Someone dives in.

If you jump too, turn to page 109.

If you stick with the raft, turn to page 112.

You decide to stick with setting off the rockets. Many lives may depend on you now.

Jessica sets a rocket in its launcher. You fix the detonator on it. Jessica counts silently.

"Go now!" she says.

You pull the cord that fires the detonator.

That ship should have responded by now to the rockets and the Morse light Jessica flashes into the night. So far, it shows no sign that it's seen the *Titanic*'s signals.

"I guess all we can do is keep setting off these rockets and wait," Jessica says.

At least they're exciting to watch, you think, as they spill light across the dark sea.

The End

You and McCracken tie the raft to a couple of cargo rings on deck.

The *Titanic* lurches forward into the water. The horrendous sound of heavy metal tearing apart rises from beneath you in the hold. The deck shudders under your feet. Muffled snapping sounds boom from inside the ship.

"There she goes," shouts McCracken. "Sounds like she's breaking in half!"

Turn to page 100.

100

To your amazement, the *Titanic*'s stern settles back almost level. As the ship quiets you hear people within it screaming and shouting.

A mass of people rush from the third-class entrance aft of the well deck. They cling to the railings, the aft bridge supports, and the poop deck cargo cranes. Some start climbing down into the well deck toward the raft.

Once again the deck tips. Again the stern begins to poke vertically into the sky. The lights flick off, come back on glowing dull red, then die.

Go on to the next page.

It's so dark. You didn't plan on the lights going out! Icy water swirls around your feet.

You yelp at the shock of the cold, then shout, "McCracken, cut the raft loose! I can't find my knife. I think the ship's going down!"

You glimpse the dim shapes of bodies falling. Several people have slid down the well deck and bumped up against the raft.

"I can't," yells McCracken. "Someone knocked my knife out of my hand. Jump for it!" He wades away along the horizontal well-deck bulkhead.

You don't let go. The stern is pointing straight up in the air; the water is up to your knees. A calm comes over you now that the water has reached you. Maybe you're just numb. You want to try untying the raft, even though it seems useless. You've got just seconds to act.

If you swim for your life, turn to page 105.

If you try to untie the raft in the rising water, turn to page 102.

The deck is poised above you, nearly vertical. You grab at the knots of the raft, as the stern of the *Titanic* pivots under you and rises into the air for the final plunge.

You look up, awestruck. The stern looks like a giant black castle as it towers above you, poking toward the gleaming stars. Something from the poop deck bridge crashes next to you, showering you with an icy spray. The raft rights itself and floats free for a moment. You scramble up onto it.

Frantically you struggle with the knots and get one untied. You grab for the last line that's still tied. The knot jerks tight under your fingers and disappears underwater. The black wall of the stern is gliding straight down alongside the raft—and pulling it and you underwater!

Turn to page 104.

You hang on underwater, stars flashing behind your eyes from the icy shock of the water over your head.

Something lets go with a ripping vibration. The raft pops up to the surface with you clinging to it. You're thirty feet from the *Titanic*'s stern, finally clear of it as it glides below the surface.

A weak voice calls to you. It's McCracken. You drag his body onto the raft. He can't talk. After a while he just lies still.

Other people struggle to climb on the raft. You're too numb and weak to help them much. Most of those who succeed lie motionless like McCracken.

As dawn breaks, you notice a ship far in the distance pulling up people from the *Titanic*'s lifeboats. A few hours later, another ship steams slowly back and forth through the bits and pieces of the *Titanic*'s wreckage.

The ship is so close you can almost make out the name on its side. You try yelling, but your voice is too weak to carry. When you try to stand and wave your arms, you stumble and fall into the water. It takes precious minutes and all your strength to regain the raft. By then the ship has begun to steam away. You hold onto the hope that there will be another one. And soon.

The End

You try to wade over the well-deck bulkhead but the water is so deep that your feet can't touch. You just swim for it, away from the foundering stern. You breathe in short gasps, the icy air stinging your lungs, the cold water cramping your body. You're too scared to look back at the immense sinking hulk that is now the *Titanic*.

In the dim starlight, something looms out of the smooth black water. With already numb fingers, you reach for it, gasping from the cold. It's a bunch of deck chairs, still in a nested stack. By crawling on them and balancing carefully, you manage to keep most of your body out of the freezing water. You have to lie perfectly still to keep your balance. The sea remains calm and smooth.

After a while, you can no longer hear the shouts and cries of people in life belts around you. You're not sure whether they've fallen silent or whether you are just drifting into unconsciousness. It makes no difference to you.

A lifeboat appears and voices call. You struggle to raise your head. Strong hands hoist you into the boat. In a miraculous recovery, after a couple of minutes of shaking your legs and waving your arms, you feel strong enough to help row.

The End

106

"Let's wait it out. The water's almost here," you say. McCracken shrugs but nods his agreement.

The *Titanic*'s bow is now underwater. The ship's going down by the bow, and slowly its stern rises.

The raft leans against the angle of the well deck. Off both sides of the stern, lifeboats move slowly away from the *Titanic;* in the bright lights they glow white against the smooth black water. The people in the lifeboats appear to be having trouble rowing.

"Doesn't the *Titanic* have crew who know how to row?" you ask McCracken.

"Reckon there's a few boatmen, but I'm sure none of 'em made it into that boat," he says with a grin.

Freezing cold water swirls over your feet, bringing you both back to reality.

"Wow, cold!" you shout. "McCracken, we've got to get this raft over now! Can you find help? Maybe there are some people still down in third class. Tell them all the lifeboats are gone."

McCracken scrambles up the deck and disappears into the third-class entrance.

A moment later, a crowd pours out of the entrance; some are brave enough to slide down to the raft.

"No one told us! We didn't know the ship was sinking."

Go on to the next page.

A boy about your age and a group of several men, some speaking languages you've never heard, lift and slide the raft through the water of the steeply sloping deck. Stupendous grinding and crashing sounds shake the deck beneath you.

To your surprise, the deck suddenly levels off, and the *Titanic*'s stern settles back on the water. At the same time, the water drains from the deck, and the sea is again ten feet beneath the deck rail.

"Look, she floats again!" a man says in an Italian accent. He's grinning.

"She's breaking in two!" yells McCracken. "This stern'll sink like a stone in a couple of minutes."

Turn to page 108.

108

You and McCracken motion to the men to lift the raft over the rail. The two of you loop lines tied to the raft around the railing and try to lower it gently to the water.

The raft swings away from you. Your left hand is crushed between the railing and the line. The raft lands in the water intact and you jump aboard. Some people follow; some cling in fear to the sinking ship.

Late the next morning, the surgeon onboard the *Carpathia*, which has picked up you and the other *Titanic* survivors, tells you your hand will heal, but you'll never play the piano again. Your brilliant musical career has ended, but at least you're alive.

The End

With a yell, you dive away from the upended ship. The freezing water feels like razor blades slashing your skin.

You swim underwater as far as you can and then start to surface. A strong current sucks you back down. It pins you against what feels like wire mesh. An image of a ventilation screen on the deck flashes through your panicked mind. You push away with all your strength; a moment later the water pouring into the ship through the screen pins you against it again.

Just as your lungs feel like they're about to explode, a bubble of warm air puffs through the screen and gently frees you. But it's too late. The ship has pulled you far underwater.

The next time you'll be seen will be decades into the future, when an undersea robot records the image of your skeleton, one finger extended to point at the sunken bag of Andrew's gold.

The End

It reminds you of the Fourth of July. You look at your watch. It's 12:45 A.M., an hour since the *Titanic* struck the iceberg.

"That's your answer, miss," the seaman says. "She's signaling for help—any help—now."

"Do you suppose they've seen something?" you ask. You stand and scan the horizon with your binoculars.

To the north, you sight some lights. "Look, ship lights!" you shout.

The seaman confirms your find. "Looks like a steamer—two lights, one on her foremast, the other on her main mast. And it looks like she's headed this way."

If you suggest heading for the ship, turn to page 120.

If you want to wait near the well-lit Titanic *for the ship to come to you, turn to page 114.*

You stay calm, fascinated by the spectacle of the great ship's stern blocking the stars.

"Let's paddle, all together. Go!" you say. The raft moves a few feet from the ship's vertical side. The *Titanic* is sinking so slowly and evenly that the only mark of motion is a ring of white foam around the boat. Clusters of people cling to the ship, then drop off into the sea, screaming. Only a few make it to the raft.

"Look at that fellow," Jessica says. A man is calmly picking his way onto the stern plates as they rise. He's balancing himself perfectly, standing straight up above the stern railing. Always finding the level, he rides the stern straight down out of the night sky. The stern disappears with a gurgling sound and the man calmly steps off into the water as though he were getting out of an elevator.

"It's the chief baker," you say, and throw him a rope. You pull him up onto the raft.

He recognizes you. "Sorry I didn't bring any bread. But I do have this." He reaches into his hip pocket and passes around a box of chocolate candies.

Shortly after dawn, a ship picks you up. Andrew and his friend give you a check for five thousand dollars later that day. You use it to buy the grand piano of your dreams.

The End

You decide it's safer to stick close to your mother ship. Another rocket goes off from the *Titanic*'s bridge. That steamer's got to see these distress signals, you think.

An hour passes. The steamer's lights disappear, and more lifeboats join you in the dark water. Some of them are full; others are only half full. The boats group not far from the *Titanic*, like children afraid to leave a parent. The *Titanic*'s bow steadily sinks under the water. The decks and portholes are still ablaze with lights. The boat looks like a vast

palace that's askew and tipping. All the lifeboats have left the ship now, and masses of people swarm back toward the stern to escape the black water welling up into the ship's submerging decks.

Fascinated, you all watch the horrifying, gradual disappearance of the ship. The entire forward well deck is underwater. Toward the bow you see portholes still gleaming under it. The *Titanic* looks eerily beautiful, like a supernatural sea creature glowing underwater.

Turn to page 116.

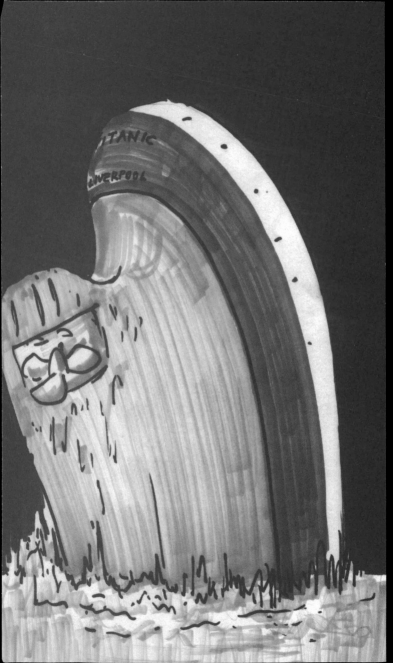

Steeper and steeper the ship cants downward into the sea. A roar from inside, like tons of gravel and rocks running down a steel chute, sweeps across the water. The engines and all moveable interior parts—boilers, coal, freight, pianos, and furniture—are crashing toward the bow. The first funnel, and then the second, come smashing down into the water in a spray of red sparks and steam. Over half the length of the ship is underwater now. Higher and steeper the stern rises, all lights aglow. Then the lights go out, and you're alone in the dark. Cracking sounds as sharp as cannon shots resound clearly across the water. The *Titanic* breaks in two between the third and fourth funnels and sparks from the tearing, shearing metal dance into the water. The whole forward two-thirds of the ship sinks.

For a few minutes, the aft third of the *Titanic* levels as though it has stopped sinking. In a moment the broken end sinks into the water as well, and the stern points higher and higher until it stands vertical. The words TITANIC LIVERPOOL point straight up to the stars. With hundreds of people clinging to rails, stanchions, and ventilators, the remaining section of the ship descends straight down like a gliding elevator. Gone!

Turn to page 118.

A sigh seems to go up from the water surrounding the sinking ship. It's echoed by gasps from the lifeboats standing by.

A shouting, crying chorus of voices swells louder and louder as the ship disappears and darkness returns.

"Oh Lord, it's people in the water," a voice says behind you.

"They look like floating seagulls," another says.

"It's their white life belts," you say. "Let's see if we can rescue some of them. We're only half full."

"They'll freeze to death in this water in a half hour or less," says one of the crew members. "But there aren't enough lifeboats for everybody."

"They'll swamp our boat," shouts a passenger. "Then we'll all die, freezing in that water!"

Go on to the next page.

"We can't just leave them to drown or freeze to death," says a woman at an oar beside you.

"Let's row," you say. The two of you start, and the seaman at the tiller turns the boat toward the mass of people in the water yelling for help. The other two people at the oars refuse to row at first, then make feeble rowing motions. Even not rowing very hard, it's easy to cover the six hundred yards back to the floating survivors.

It's a gory sight. There are so many people in the water. There must be hundreds and hundreds, you think. As you near the struggling bodies, you worry about the boat being swamped with those trying to climb aboard. But people are so frozen after a few minutes in the water, they have no strength to hold on to the boat, much less swamp it. In fact, it's exhausting work trying to get a full load of swimmers over the three-foot-high sides of the lifeboat. Their soaked clothes and bulky life belts make it slow going.

Most of the rescued lie in the bottom of the lifeboat, moaning. Some are very still and appear frozen.

At last, someone on your boat begins to row toward the other lifeboats. You and the seamen are worn out from the work. Dawn is breaking and a wind begins to blow.

A shout goes up from some boats in the distance. Your binoculars show a steamer making speed in your direction. She's sending up rockets to show she's seen you. Rescue!

Turn to page 49.

"Let's row toward the boat. Look, the *Titanic* is signaling again," you say. Another rocket booms off the ship's bridge. "That ship's got to notice."

"Right. Let's pull for her then," says the seaman. The one other crewman aboard from the *Titanic* nods. "No one's going to help us but ourselves."

Rowing is hard work, but it keeps you from freezing in the cold air. In fact, you get so hot you give your coat to a shivering man.

"We're not getting any closer to that ship," you say, peering through your binoculars at the ship's lights.

A few minutes pass. "I think that steamer is going away," says the seaman. "All I see is her stern light. It's getting fainter."

The lifeboat is now miles from the *Titanic*. About half an hour ago, the *Titanic* stopped sending up distress rockets. It looks like the boat is moving away, but you know it's sinking. You feel panic thinking you're going to be left alone in this tiny lifeboat. The other people in the lifeboat are also full of doubts.

"Let's turn back."

"We should have stayed with the other lifeboats."

"We're lost!"

Everybody's shouting now.

All the lights from the *Titanic* wink out. The strange steamer's lights are fading. It doesn't seem to matter much what you do now.

Turn to page 122.

122

The White Star Line hires several ships to search the sea for bodies. Three weeks later one of these ships finds lifeboat No. 7 still floating, but with no survivors on board.

The End

CREDITS

Illustrator: Sittisan Sundaravej (Quan). Sittisan is a resident of Bangkok, Thailand and an old fan of *Choose Your Own Adventure*. He attended The University of the Arts in Philadelphia, where he received his BSc. in Architecture and a BFA for Animation. He has been a 2D and 3D animation director for productions in Asia and the United States and is a freelance illustrator.

Illustrator: Kriangsak Thongmoon (Tao). Kriangsak is a graphic artist living in Thailand. After attending Srinakarinwiroj Prasarnmitr University in Bangkok, Kriangsak made a career illustrating for various well-known publications in Thailand before switching his concentrations to 3D modeling and computer animation. However, his love for drawing and sketching still keeps him coming back to non-computer generated illustrations.

Cover Illustrator: Nathan Barchus Originally from Connecticut, Nate recently graduated with a B.F.A. in Illustration from the Rhode Island School of Design. He studied primarily painting and drawing techniques with a focus on the figure. His works are primarily in oil on canvas and digital media.

ABOUT THE AUTHOR

Jim Wallace lived in Norway for a year and taught school in Kampala, Uganda, for three years. He also worked in Tokyo teaching English and writing English language textbooks. He likes to ride Italian motorcycles. He also enjoys chainsawing wood on his property in Vermont. For some time he's pursued photography and has exhibited his work in Vermont. He lives in Montpelier and has a 12-year-old son.

**For games, activities and other fun stuff,
or to write to Jim Wallace, visit us
online at CYOA.com**

ADVENTURER'S LOG

ADVENTURER'S LOG

ADVENTURER'S LOG

ADVENTURER'S LOG

ADVENTURER'S LOG

ADVENTURER'S LOG

Look for New Titles

CHOOSE YOUR OWN ADVENTURE® 36

PUNISHMENT: EARTH

CHOOSE FROM 15 ENDINGS!

NEW COVER LOOK!

BY R. A. MONTGOMERY